This book belongs to:

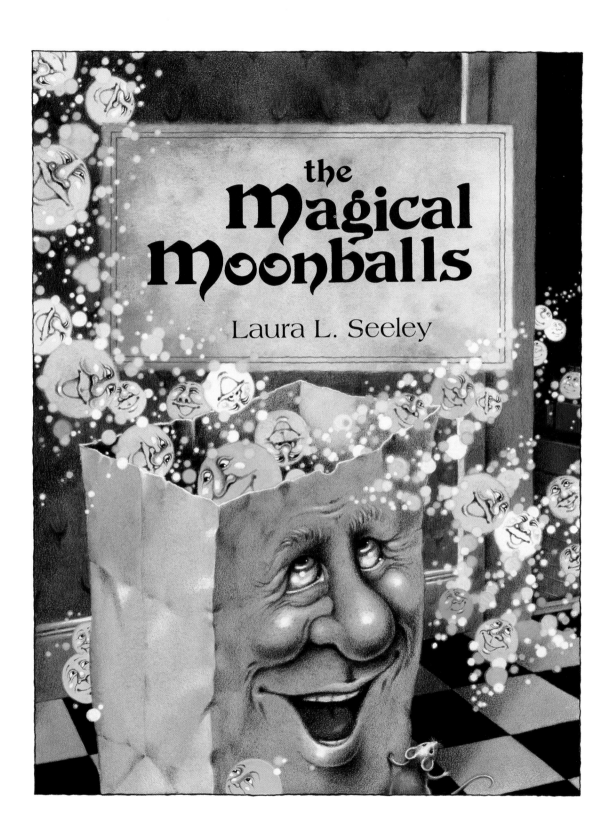

the Magical Moonballs

Laura L. Seeley

PEACHTREE PUBLISHERS, LTD.
Atlanta

Published by
PEACHTREE PUBLISHERS, LTD.
494 Armour Circle NE
Atlanta, Georgia 30324

Book design by Candace J. Magee and Laura L. Seeley

Printed in Mexico
10 9 8 7 6 5 4 3 2 1

Library of Congress Cataloging-in-Publication Data
Seeley, Laura L.
    The magical moonballs / Laura L. Seeley.
      p. cm.
    ISBN 1-56145-189-4
      [1. Moon—Fiction. 2. Smile—Fiction. 3. Stories in rhyme.]
I. Title
PZ8.3.S452Mag   1992
[E]—dc20   92-16698
                                        CIP
                                        AC

the Magical Moonballs

Dedicated to
CARY EISENBERG,
who gave me the spark,
lots of smiles,
and the drafting table.

With appreciation to:
GAIL SEELEY
for her help as the family editor
and for being the ever-supportive mom.

PAUL SEELEY
for some very candid art direction.

ANDREW FENLON *and* **GERALD GRAIG**
for their inspiration and editorial assistance.

KATE SEELEY *and* **LINDA SEELEY**
for their support and suggestions
as sister and sister-in-law.

NICK PETTY *and* **TERRY KAY**
for sharing their inspiring whims.

DAVID SEELEY
for his cool concepting on the moonballs mobile.

MICHELLE JOBE, PHILIP SACCO,
RUSSELL SHAW, BILLY CRISP,
KÄTHE DOUGLAS, GARY BUCKLES,
and **KATHRYN CLARK**
for their helpful hints
and various useful tidbits.

and to
EMILY WRIGHT *and* **LAURIE EDWARDS,**
Peachtree Publishers' articulate editors,
who on several occasions
sweated with me over this manuscript.

Have you ever had thoughts
about make-believe things
such as hotdogs with faces
or flowers with wings?

Is the man in the moon
really made of Swiss cheese?
Just who does he smile at?
. . . Suppose he could sneeze!

Imagine a gift
he might send to all places
that shines through a moonball
and spreads across faces.

'Tis a gift we all have
that can grow when we share it,
. . . the gift of a smile,
and you just can't compare it.

It comes in all colors
and starts anywhere,
making everyday magic
that moves through the air.

For some fantasy fun
it is you we invite
to watch millions of moonballs
begin their next flight. . . .

The man in the moon
drifted slowly in space
as he looked down below
with a smile on his face.

But he seemed a bit sad
from this lonesome lifestyle.
Not a soul was out there
to send back a smile.

Though he longed for a friend
there was no one in sight,
so he spent his days daydreaming,
even at night.

Yet his eyes always twinkled
while nothing else stirred. . . .
Then on one cloudy night
something funny occurred.

His nose felt an itch,
and it twitched in the breeze.
Then he shuddered and shivered
and sneezed a big sneeze!

~**2**~

With sparkling colors
the clouds burst away
into magical moonballs
who wanted to play.

They tumbled in teams,
full of frolicking fun,
for their mystical journey
had now just begun.

Some houses below
could hear faint, distant cries. . . .
There were squeals full of happiness
up in the skies!

It looked like a make-believe
moonlit snowfall
as these messengers came,
bringing smiles to them all.

With spry somersaults,
laughing out with delight,
down the chimneys they spilled
in a rush of moonlight.

A fireplace heard
these unusual sounds
while the logs watched them enter
in quick leaps and bounds.

Some bricks held their breath
as the moonballs flew in,
while a lamp said, "Hello!"
and lit up with a grin.

As soon as the moons
had arrived in great numbers
things quickly began
to awake from their slumbers.

The three vases mumbled
some sleepy protests,
but they soon laughed along
with these little house guests.

The couch cushions woke
while the stereo snored.
Then she switched herself on
as the moonballs explored.

The candle flames danced
to the stereo's tunes
while the musical notes
did a waltz with the moons.

The grandfather clock
chimed his bells to the song
when a bunch of old books
started singing along.

The moonballs sang with them
then pranced up the wall,
heading high for the ceiling
and out to the hall.

Into the kitchen
they gleefully started.
Then along with a teapot
they danced and they darted.

Slipping and sliding
across the floor tiles,
they woke the whole room
'til it filled up with smiles.

A cup in a saucer
looked up in surprise
while the salt and the pepper
wiped sleep from their eyes.

A cookie jar coughed,
popping out macaroons
while a dish did the jig
with two forks and two spoons.

A pair of potholders
had fun with a group
of bananas, fudge brownies,
and four cans of soup.

The bananas jumped over
the table and chairs,
spilling apples, some grapes,
and a trio of pears.

The fruit tapped a dance
with a striped rolling pin
while some mugs did the twist
with a blue coffee tin.

The fridge asked the moonballs
to come on inside,
where they circled the milkjug
and made him cross-eyed.

The bacon and eggs
formed a breakfast parade
while the grape jelly followed
the peach marmalade.

The moonballs kept up
with their teases and tickles
on twenty-one meatballs
and seven dill pickles.

The mustard and ketchup
enjoyed the horseplay
while some hotdogs chilled out
with a spinach soufflé.

The moons left the fridge
for a quick game of tag.
Then they played hide 'n' seek
with a brown paper bag.

Then they zigged and they zagged,
dashing out through the door
to continue this twilight
terrestrial tour.

From the kitchen they came,
kicking off a moonrace
as they chased one another
right up the staircase.

They made happy sounds
as they whisked by the walls,
rousing dreamers upstairs
with their giggles and calls.

The bathroom door squeaked
when he heard the commotion,
which woke up the towels
and tissues and lotion.

The toothbrushes laughed
in this strange atmosphere
as the moonballs streamed in,
full of chuckles and cheer.

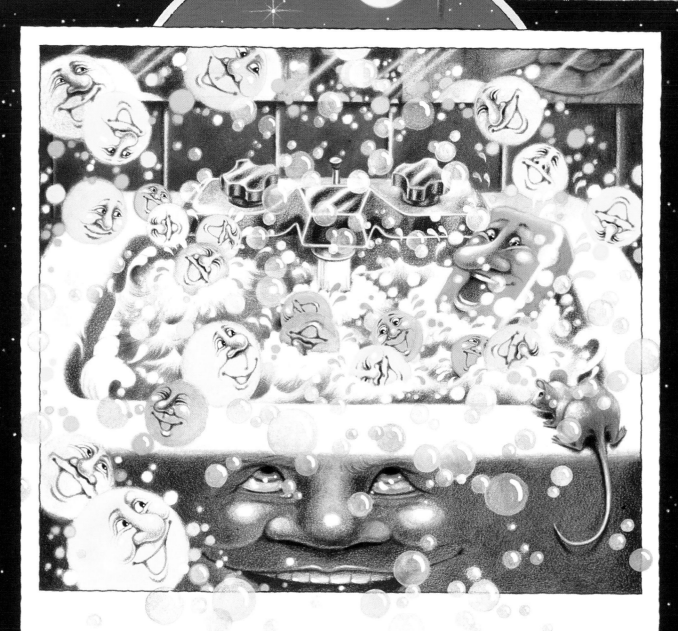

In shimmering showers
they fell to the sink,
so he filled up with water
to give them a drink.

But they plunged with a splash,
taking dips by the doubles,
then swam with the soap
'til the sink brimmed with bubbles.

A sprinkle of smiles
brightened up every face
as this magical mood
spread all over the place.

When a cup bumped the mirror
and saw her reflection,
she scared herself off
in a different direction.

She twirled all around
in a terrible tizzy,
then danced with two ducks
'til they all became dizzy.

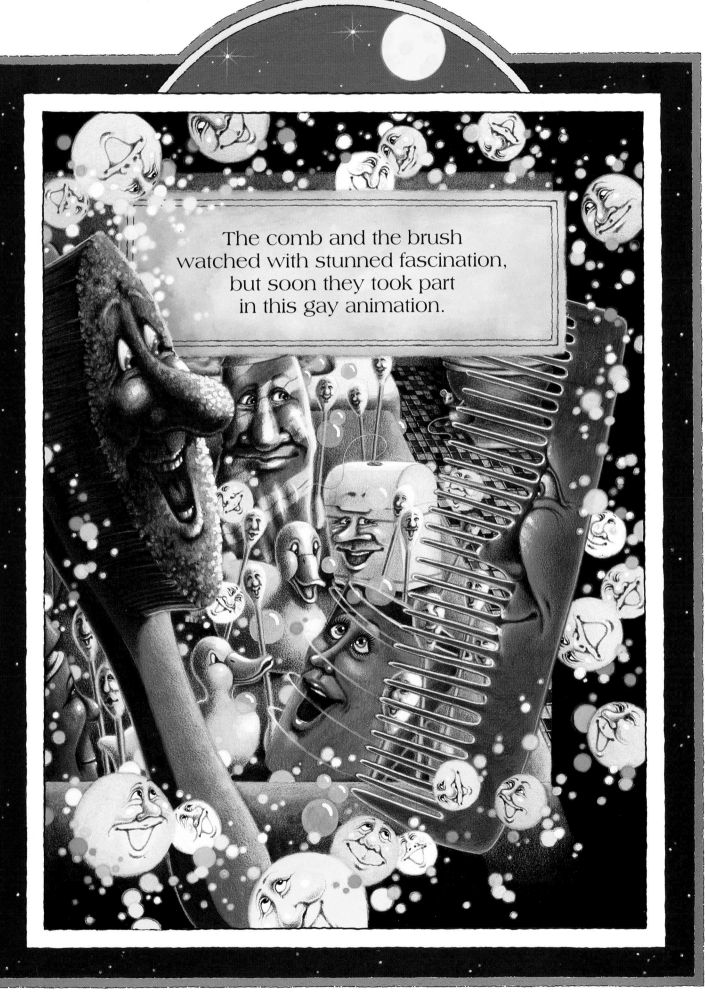

The comb and the brush
watched with stunned fascination,
but soon they took part
in this gay animation.

They startled some sneakers
and shook up some shoes,
gently pulling their laces,
disturbing their snooze.

The moonballs spun circles
around the bedposts,
where they spooked an old painting,
like little, round ghosts.

With some dolls and a train
they raced under the covers
and pounced on the pillows,
like frisky fun-lovers.

Their pranks caught the eye
of the drawers and sweatsocks
while the clock cheered them on
with excited "tick tocks!"

A teddybear woke
from his teddybear nap
as the moonballs approached
and hopped right in his lap!

He snuggled back into
the overstuffed chair,
and they both watched in awe
with a hypnotized stare.

When the bear caught a moonball
and held up his arm,
all the wallpaper flowers
fell under its charm.

So the moonballs cruised up
toward the wallpaper flowers,
who watched them show off
with their magical powers.

The wallflowers blushed
at these marvelous things. . . .
Then a flower flew off
with her painted leaf-wings.

She thought she was dreaming
and started to blink
'til a moon looked her way
with a smile and a wink.

She followed the moonballs,
then uttered a sigh. . . .
Through the window they went,
and she whispered, "Good-bye."

One by one they slipped out
full of final "Farewells!"
leaving faces of friendliness
under their spells.

Toward the rooftop they rose
for the end of their flight,
as their trip would be over
before the daylight.

Tonight they had finished
their mission with style,
having brought down a message
from one lonely smile.

The moonballs took off,
sailing further away
as a glow in the east
dawned another new day.

Their echoes of laughter
were almost defined
in the trails made of moondust
they left far behind. . . .

The man in the moon
is not truly alone,
for his tireless strength
is a smile etched in stone.

It really is magic
how spirits can lift
from just one lifted spirit
and one simple gift.

So

When you notice sad faces
and see what they lack,
send a smile their way—
it's the gift that comes back.

And maybe it won't
(there are no guarantees),
but it *could* be contagious,
you know . . . like a sneeze.